Tap it in

Written by Pranika Sharma

Collins

Tim pats it.

pat pat pat

Dan tips it.

tap tap tap

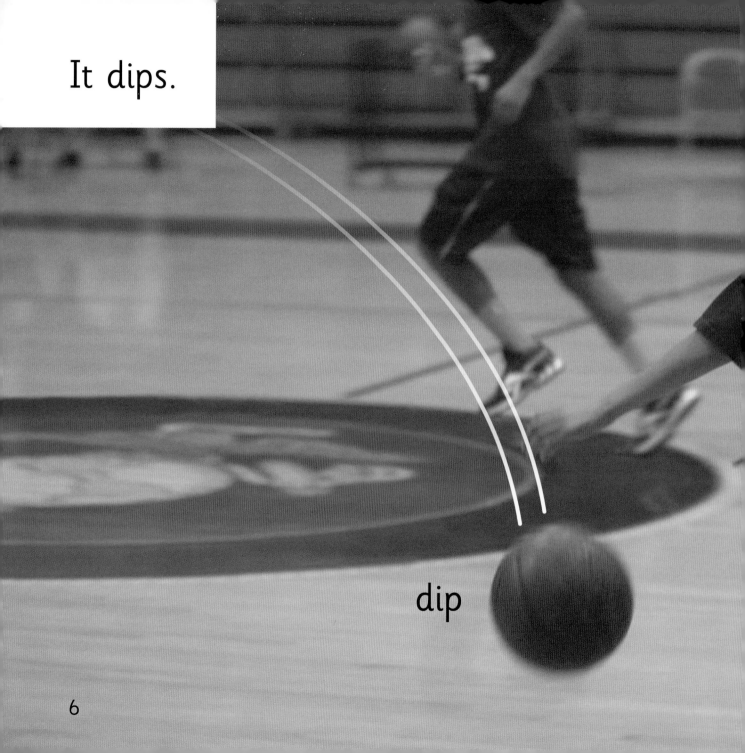

It dips.

dip

Pam pads in.

It taps.

tap

Sam nips in.

Sid nips in.

Pat it Nat.

It tips in.

Pip did it.

After reading

Letters and Sounds: Phase 2

Word count: 36

Focus phonemes: /s/ /a/ /t/ /p/ /i/ /n/ /m/ /d/

Curriculum links: Physical development

Early learning goals: Reading: read and understand simple sentences; use phonic knowledge to decode regular words and read them aloud accurately

Developing fluency

- Your child may enjoy hearing you read the book.
- Take turns to read a page aloud. Demonstrate reading with enthusiasm to make the game sound exciting.

Phonic practice

- Turn to page 2. Ask your child to sound out the letters in the name **Tim**. (t/i/m – **Tim**)
- On pages 8–9, focus on the words **taps** and **nips**. Ask your child to sound out and blend each word, checking they don't muddle the sounds /a/ in **taps** and /i/ in **nips**.
- Look at the "I spy sounds" pages (14 and 15). Point to and sound out the /m/ at the top of page 14, then point to the medal the girl is wearing and the man is giving and say "medal", emphasising the /m/ sound. Ask your child to find other things that start with the /m/ sound. (*mum, man, mop, mouse, melon, mug, moon, milk*).

Extending vocabulary

- Turn to page 9. Ask your child: What word could we use instead of **nips**? (e.g. *runs, dashes, rushes*) Ask your child to test out their ideas by reading the sentence with their word replacing **nips**. Does it make sense?